Christian Version

A focus on changing attitudes within the family.
A children's story with a counseling session.

The Secret of the Amazing Zoo

by
Mona L. Moubarek

Published by
Glorybound Publishing
Las Vegas, Nevada
2014

Secret of the Amazing Zoo

© Copyright Mona Moubarek 2014
Published by GBK (Glorybound Kids Books)
Subsidiary of Glorybound Publishing
SAN 256-4564
10 9 8 7 6 5 4 3 2
Second Edition/ First Printing
Printed in the United States of America
ISBN 978-1-60789-5 1-60789-572-2
KDP ISBN 9781085856621
Copyright data is available on file.

Moubarek, Mona, 1961-
        Secret of the Amazing Zoo/Mona Moubarek
        Includes biographical reference.
1. Children's Book   2. Parenting Helps
I. Title

www.gloryboundpublishing.com

Heart to Heart Books

This set of books focuses on nurturing sturdy spiritual and emotional values within children and families. They give building blocks for healthy relationships targeting what is most important deep down within the heart. Many books come with counseling manuals.

Secret of the Amazing Zoo was originally written in 2001 being released in 2013. The book grew with Mona growing into the talents to fully illustrate the original story. Since its inception, she developed needed skills to illustrate the entire book using the techniques in Photoshop and Illustrator computer programs. Lora is Veronica, Mona's daughter with some minor enhancements added to make her character fit in the book. Many of the original pictures were adaptations from frequent trips to parks and the Las Angeles Zoo. After hours and hours; days and months of training, Mona is very happy to release her first book, Secret of the Amazing Zoo. We would be remiss not to mention Sheri Hauser, her publisher, aided in the development of her skills pouring over the art pixil by pixil until it became what it is. We are proud to release Secret of the Amazing Zoo which will be immediately followed by the Arabic Language translated edition (by Mona, of course).

****

Summary of the Book Secret of the Amazing Zoo

Pride in our attitude affects our actions towards life. In the book, Lora goes through a big challenge at the zoo and realizes she needs to give up her pride and change her attitude. This challenge is a stepping stone for her to become a more loving and kind person making her personality to be the best it can be.

This is a story about girl named Lora, who lived with her Mom and Dad, her younger brother, Zack, and their little dog, named Alex. Lora was a very angry girl who yelled at everybody, even Alex. One day she visited a very special place where she learned an important lesson and she never yelled at anybody ever again.

One Saturday Lora had nothing to do, so she decided to go the zoo. It was not far from her house, so she set out walking and soon found herself standing in front of a huge door painted with rainbow colors. As she stood there trying to figure out how to open the door, it suddenly opened. She took a few steps inside, but saw no one there, only enclosures with different kinds of animals in them.

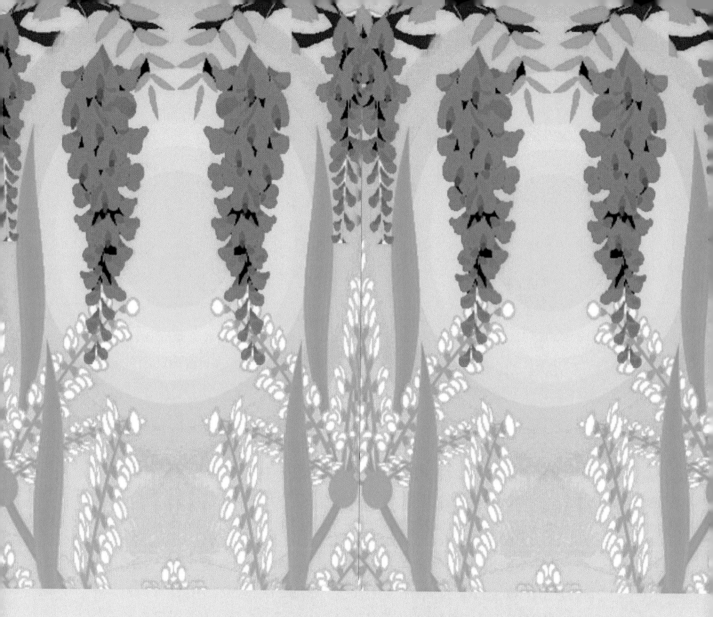

There were monkeys in the first cage, jumping around and making noises to welcome her. Lora looked at the monkeys and said, "You are too noisy and you look silly when you jump around your cage."

She moved on to the next enclosure where she saw two giraffes quietly eating leaves from the tops of a very tall tree. "How funny-looking you are with your long necks."

Next to the giraffes was a duck pond.
Five ducks swam round and round
quacking loudly and having lots of fun.

"Why are you making so much
noise?" Shouted Lora. "I don't like it."

Lora went to the zebra's cage and looked at them angrily. She then went from cage to cage visiting all of the animals – rabbits, dogs, and cats. All of the animals waved at Lora in their own special way to welcome her to the amazing zoo. Lora got angry with every animal because she did not want them to wave at her. She decided it was time to go home. As she turned to leave, the animals started singing a goodbye song. That made her angry too.

"Stop singing! I don't like your song and I don't like any of you," she shouted.

Lora ran back to the door, but no matter how hard she tried, she couldn't open it. She thought about it for a minute before she figured out the answer. She would need the animals to help her. "I'd better be nice, humble and make friends with them so they will help me open the door," she said.

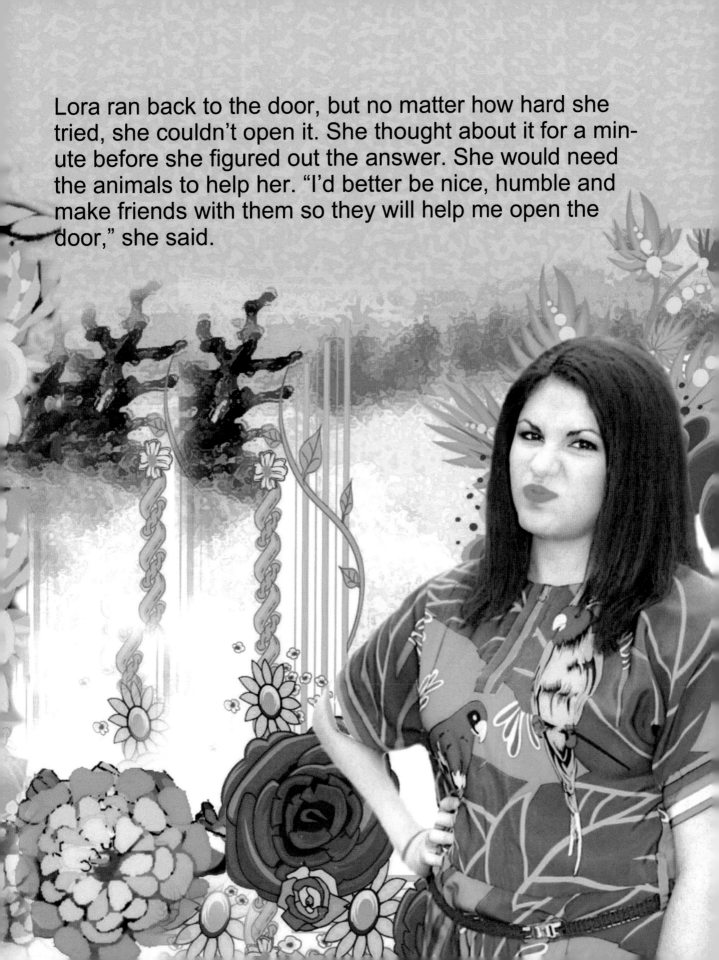

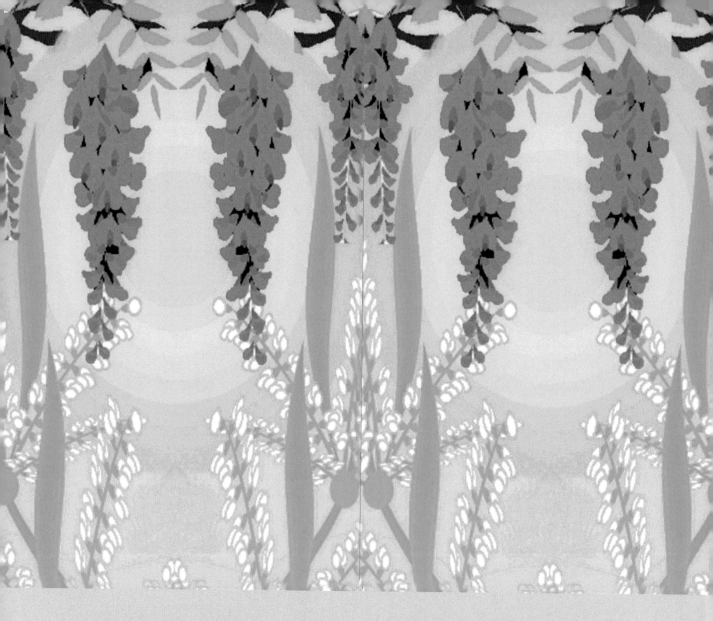

She went back to the monkeys' cage and smiled at the monkeys. "You are very cute when you jump. I like the happy sounds you make too," she told them. "Will you be my friend?"

One monkey smiled and gave her a few of his hairs. "Put them in your pocket," he told her.

"Thank you," she said and put the hairs in her pocket.

Next she went to the giraffes' enclosure and smiled at them. "What beautiful, long necks you have, just right for reaching the high branches," she said. "Will you be my friend?"

One giraffe allowed Lora to pet him. "Because you are being nice, we will give you some of our hair."

Lora did not understand why
all of the animals wanted to
give her some of their hair,
but she took it and put it in her
pocket. "Thank you," she said.
Lora went to the zebra's cage
and gave them a big smile.

By now, Lora was very hungry
and tired.

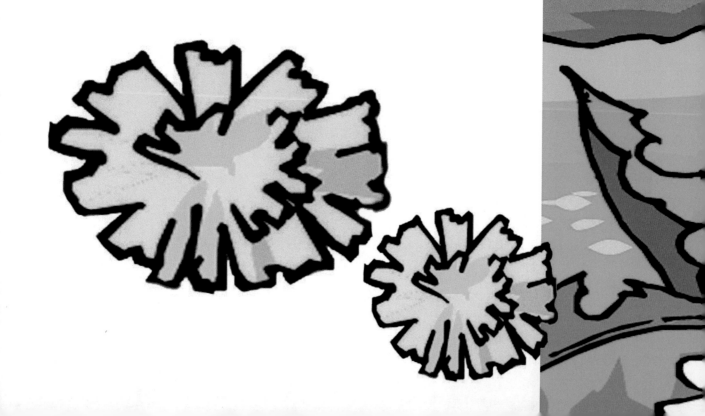

She decided to visit the zoo's garden to find something to eat before visiting the rest of the animals. She stood in front of the garden door, but could not figure out how to open it. Then she heard a voice say, "You cannot come into the garden unless you drop the animals' hair through the little window." Lora dropped the hair inside and the door opened.

Inside was a beautiful garden filled with yummy fruits and vegetables. Lora selected a sweet, juicy apple and sat down to eat it. When she finished eating, she looked around at all of the flowers and trees and other plants. She enjoyed being in the garden very much.

As she was leaving the garden, she saw that the rainbow entry door was open just a little, but she decided to visit the ducks and the other animals before she went home. Lora went to every enclosure and told all of them how lovely and kind they were and thanked them for being her friend.

Every time Lora said something nice and petted the animals, the rainbow door opened a little wider. She was so busy helping them clean their cages and bringing them fresh water to drink that she didn't see that the rainbow door was wide open and she could go home.

Lora suddenly realized that the secret of the rainbow door and the garden door was showing love and kindness to others, and being humble. She was happy to discover the secret, but she was not quite ready to leave. She went back to each enclosure and told each animal, "I love you!"

She walked around the amazing zoo, singing this song –

"What beautiful friends you are,

What lovely creatures God has made,

I will miss you every day until I see you again."

When Lora finished her song, the rainbow door was standing wide open. She hurried home and as soon as she arrived, she gave everyone a big hug – even Alex.

HEART TO HEART

HEART TO HEART
- A Family Discussion

This section is meant for the parents/teachers and their children to read together and discuss.

We don't only see things with our eyes, but also with our attitude.

What does it mean to have a negative or positive attitude?

Well Let's First Start With a Story to Explain the Meaning of Attitude:

Situations can be seen in different ways according to our attitude.
When I was a little girl, I would visit the beach every year. One time, my dad told me a story that is very relevant to attitudes.

There was a fisherman whose house faced the ocean. One day he took his boat and went fishing. Suddenly, the waves flipped the boat. The fisherman desperately called out for help. Some people heard him, and they came and saved his life. After they saved him, he went home and asked a friend if he could help him block the window that looked out at the ocean. Every time he looked through that window, he remembered the awful danger that he had faced. His friend looked at him and said you should ask me to make this window wider, because every time you look at the ocean you will remember the great miracle and rejoice. Here, there were two people and each one looked at this situation with a different attitude.

What Does it Mean to Have a Negative or Positive Attitude?

Attitude is how we reply and react to what is happening.

Negative and Positive Attitudes:

A negative attitude is when we allow the wrong choices to direct us, such as pride, anger, greed, fear, rejection, dishonesty, disrespect, low self-esteem, gossip, etc. On the other hand, a positive attitude is a good attitude. It's when we choose love, kindness; honesty, trust, joy, and respect to direct us.

We are going to talk about different attitudes in life.

Attitude of Pride:

Humility is not putting you down or feeling unworthy. It makes you look at your strong points and say, "God gives me these strong points. I did not give them to myself. I give the glory to God. Second, he gave them to me as a responsibility to help those who have weak points, not to reject them."

Pride is when I put the cup above the water tap, and nothing fills the cup. It is like saying that you know more than everyone and no one can teach you anything. Humility, however, is when we put the cup under the water to be filled. Pride is also when people cannot say, "Sorry." Pride is when we feel superior (look high upon ourselves), while looking down upon others. Pride ultimately is when we control others. The attitude of pride causes us to judge people without seeing our own mistakes. It also hinders us from seeing the good things in other people's lives.

Do you focus on seeing the spots and dirt that are on your brother's hand? Do you judge him with a prideful attitude? Instead, hold his hands with a loving heart, and take him to the fountain to wash his hands to set an example of a humble attitude. Pride leads us to take wrong authority over people's lives. It causes us to think that we are better than them and that we need to correct them. However, we will hurt them if we act out of a prideful attitude. We need to follow the golden rule, which tells us to do unto others as we would have them do to us.

The way we behave is a reflection of our attitudes. Jesus wants to live in us with His beautiful attitude. When we have this beautiful attitude of Christ, our family and friends will see the beauty in us and come to know Christ. Your attitude is how you look at things, not what things looks like.

It is also based on how you react; you can either react in a positive or negative way, depending on how you look at a situation. Sometimes it's easy to see other people's weak points, but hard to recognize our own.

Your Attitude at Home: (Pride)

Your attitude at home is very important. Pride causes you to hurt your family without realizing it. Humble children enjoy relationships and life. They reap the fruits of their attitude. Our attitude with our family should reflect: love, kindness, respect, humility, mercy, obedience, care, and all of the great virtues.

Stop being mean, bad-tempered, and angry at home. Quarreling, harsh words, and disliking others should have no place in your lives. Instead, be kind to each other, tenderhearted, and forgiving because you belong to Christ.

Ephesians 4: 31-32

Be completely humble and gentle; be patient, and bearing with one another in love.

Ephesians 4:2

If we have pride we will not be able to appreciate our parents or anyone in our family, no matter how hard they work for us. This negative attitude will cause us not to get along with our siblings or our friends.

When pride comes, then disgrace comes, but with humility comes wisdom.

Proverbs 29:23

Pride hinders us from respecting our siblings because we feel that we are better than them. It also hinders us from enjoying relationships or seeing the beauty in them. Love never fails, but strife and anger always fails. Your brother and sister are always friends- forever. Keep them, love them, accept them, and do not reject them because a good attitude is a sign of a mature character.

A man's pride brings him low, but a man of lowly spirit gains honor.

Proverbs 29:23

Saying Unkind Words:

Saying unkind and bad words at home is a negative attitude. It is like sitting in a messy house, full of trash. It is not a healthy or comfortable house. A great and mature person will refuse to say bad words. Choose only to say kind words. Negative words hurt and destroy. They come from an unloving heart and an immature personality. Kind words build and heal. They come from a great person and mature character. Man's words reflect who he is from the inside. Choose a healthy attitude that is full of love and kind words.

This is the reason we address pride in our lives- to create this healthy attitude and foster in a sense of well being in our lives.

Honoring Your Parents:

Honoring your parents is a great positive attitude. Choose to make great memories every day so that as the years go by, you won't have regrets. Days go by fast and they will never come back.

It is God's will to honor your parents. Fill your heart with appreciation towards your parents; this is part of having a good attitude. When your mom works hard to cook a meal say, "Thank you. I appreciate your hard work." You can even write her a note telling her how grateful you are to have a mom like her and that you love her. Do the same with your dad. Ask God to give you a tender heart towards your brother or sister. Say, "Lord, take my hard heart and give me a tender heart through your blood. Send the Holy Spirit to pour your love inside of me toward my family; and, to comfort them, encourage them, and above all not to hurt them."

Children, obey your parents in the Lord, for this is right. Honor your father and mother (which is the first commandment with a promise), that it may be well with you, and that you may live long on the earth.

Ephesians 6:1-3

I will tell you a secret. When you submit to authority like your parents, God sees that and He will take the upper hand to direct them for your good! God will do healthy things that will help you become closer to Him and keep you safe. Submit because you want to please and obey God, knowing that at the end of the narrow way is the gate of heaven. He loves us so much more than we love ourselves. He died for you and gave you Himself; therefore, He will give you, what you need if you only look to Him and trust in Him.

If your parents rebuke you, know that they do that to protect you and to teach you. As human beings, we need to be rebuked sometimes. Being rebuked helps us to create a character full of cautious actions, self control, and maturity. When your parents rebuke you, honor and respect them exactly as if they said kind words to you. Never get hurt or angry at them when they rebuke you. Instead, realize that they are raising you according to the best of their knowledge. Being rebuked help us to see the mistakes and errors that are in our ways. Good people appreciate being rebuked. Being rebuked helps you avoid a passive and careless attitude. As children, sometimes you cannot tell when something dangerous comes your way. You need the warnings of your parents to avoid those dangerous situations. Do you know why the Titanic, "the unsinkable ship," sank? The Titanic received a number of wireless messages warning about icebergs along their path. The Captain ignored these warnings. He was unaware of how serious the warnings had become. The Titanic was still steaming full speed ahead when they crashed into huge icebergs and sank. It was a horrible accident and many perished.

Do not listen to any wrong friends that have a negative influence on your life. Instead, listen to the warnings of your parents. We need to fully understand that parents have an authoritative tone of voice to protect and correct us. It is given to your parents, it is not meant for children to copy this authoritative tone and yell at one another. We have no excuse to ever yell at our brothers or sisters at home. If we do that, it will be a negative attitude that hurts and controls your siblings. Trust that you are beloved and your parents love you. Even if they do not tell you that very often, still believe in their love.

The Attitude of a Mother's Heart: IF YOU DO NOT HAVE A MOM WRITE ME AS A MOM TO YOU.

Never break your mother's heart with disobedience or disrespect. She is the first woman your eyes ever saw. Your ears heard her saying, "'I love you my child," as she gave you the first kiss and the biggest hug. You were a delightful twenty four hour occupation to her. Your joy and big smile were greater and of more worth to her than having a salary. She carried you in her arms as a baby. As you grew, she carried you in her heart. You were the center of her attention. When you were running around without realizing the dangers to protect yourself, she was there to shield you. When you fell, she carried you and kissed your wounds.

There was a time when you were little and could not say a word, but your mom's heart knew exactly what you wanted to say and what you could not say. As you grew up, she became the most faithful advisor for you to make the best choices in life. Even when you act bad and break her heart and you think that you do not deserve her love, she still never stops loving you. She is like a candle that melts to bring light to you. When you go through pain and suffering, she melts it away to provide light for you. Her actions of love cause her to melt even more. She gives herself burning and melting for you the whole journey of your life, until she gets old and finishes melting. Then she will depart; but, her marks of love will never leave. Do not break her heart.

On the entire journey, your dad has been a great support to your mom so that she could do all the wonderful things for you. If your mom asked you to take care of your younger brother or sister while she is busy doing work around the house, do it with a willing heart to honor your mother. Do not do it as a burden, but instead, use this as an enjoyable time to think of some ideas to have fun with your siblings. You need to realize that we have to help one another as a family. A united family is a strong family, but a divided family falls apart.

Fear and Respect as Attitude:

Fear and respect are important issues. We need to balance them.

It is important to respect your parents and not to be afraid of them. If you build the relationship with your parents based on fear, then you will miss out on experiencing a fulfilling sonhood and daughterhood relationships. It also makes you enjoy motherhood and fatherhood. Fear destroys this relationship and makes you feel like a slave, rather than a child. In turn, your relationship with your parents will not be healthy or fulfilling. Obedience is a choice that comes from a loving heart in the form of a good attitude. Express your feelings to your parents and ask them for ways they can help you choose to obey out of love and not out of fear. A loving child's heart is one whose is willing to obey in order to express a healthy image of the relationship between a child and their parents. There is a sweet freedom when we choose to obey out of a loving attitude and not fear.

Fear of Authority:

We also should not have fear of authority. Instead we need to have the attitude to respect authority. However, we need to be careful not to go to either extreme. The first extreme is when we have a genuine authority who corrects us in order to prevent

us from harm; but we respond to them with objections, and attack their authority. This is a wrong attitude of rebellion. The other extreme is when we have wrong people or harmful authorities who try to harm us. In this case, we have to protect ourselves by telling our parents. Never listen to any one who tells you "do not tell your parents" or "keep it secret. Put everything in the light and expose what you have heard in secret. If someone tells you that they will harm you if you tell your parents, you still need to tell your parents. Never let fear capture or harm you. Always try to be with a friend and never by yourself. Never give any personal information about yourself, or your family, to any person you do not know, even if this person appears to be a nice person. First ask your parents, because being cautious is a positive attitude.

The attitude of boldness:

When we are faced with tough actions, we repress those negative feelings because of a lack of boldness, or on the other hand, we express our feelings in a hurtful way. However, both of these attitudes are unhealthy. It is hard sometimes to have boldness with kindness. The definition of boldness is: Fearless and daring; courageous.

Learn to confidently say, "I do not like the way you talk to me. You hurt my feelings." Express your feelings without saying unkind words and be willing to forgive and let go of the hurt it caused you.

Joseph's Attitude Towards His Brothers:

Even when Joseph was in jeopardy, he kept the fear of God strongly within him.

He trusted in God through all the difficult trials he faced. His eyes were focused on God rather than on the painful situation he was in. Now, when Joseph was in a high position, he had the opportunity to revenge and punish his brothers who had cruelly wronged him. Instead, Joseph looked at God's faithfulness. Because of this, God was able to reward Joseph by using him in the time of famine.

Anyone who claims to be in the light but hates a brother or sister is still in the darkness. Anyone who loves their brother and sister lives in the light, and there is nothing in them to make them stumble. But anyone who hates a brother or sister is in the darkness and walks around in the darkness. They do not know where they are going, because the darkness has blinded them.

1 John 2:9-11

If you trust in God, He will be faithful to you like He was to Joseph.

Hurt Destroys and Demolishes the Love From The Hearts between You and Your Family:

When we repeatedly get hurt, it demolishes the love inside of us for those who have hurt us. Never let this happen. Be a leader and create unity by being ready to apologize and say you're sorry to your sister or brother.

Do not go to bed and sleep if you remember that you said bad words to your brother and sister and made him or her cry. Do not break the love in their heart towards you. Instead, say sorry to them, because being humble is a positive attitude. Hurting others is a bad attitude. Do not tell me I am going to seek revenge at her or him for what they have done to me. Instead, be a leader who is strong enough to break the wrong attitude by fixing and responding with a better attitude. Do not fix the mess with another mess to add on to it. Do not get rid of your brother because you see mistakes in him. Instead, be a leader and work with him to remove those mistakes by setting a good example for him. Because you also have flaws and everyone has weakness, let go and forgive.

The Attitude of Jealousy:

But if you have bitter jealousy and selfish ambition in your hearts, do not boast and be false to the truth.

James 3:14

For where you have envy and selfish ambition, there you find disorder and every evil practice.

James 3

The worst thing I saw in my life was jealousy- which is terrible to have in your attitude. Selfish children are jealous. They focus only on themselves in a selfish way. They always want to be the center of attention. Your attitude reflects what is in your inner heart. An attitude full of jealousy comes from an unloving heart. Selfish children focus only on loving themselves, out of an unhealthy attitude. Having an unselfish attitude does not mean to neglect or not care for yourself, or your needs, but instead, to be concerned for others, and not to prevent them from having what you have. Selfish people are not happy people. Jealousy is a sin that causes gossip. If you repent from being jealous, you will be great, mature and find happiness. You will be precious like diamonds and a great leader crossing, and stopping the mess. You will be like blossoming flowers- everyone enjoys your fragrance. When God sees your victory, He will reward you. You will be closer to His image and conquering your enemy. God puts us in situations that allow us to make mature choices. For example, if your sibling gets candy, but you do not get any and you feel like it's not fair, always remember that this situation was a test to get the jealousy out of your heart. This lesson was much more valuable than the piece of candy you missed out on. He also put you in this situation to lose your sinful nature and gain His beautiful nature. Rejoice when God puts you in these types of tests because God is maturing your character.

The person of the Holy Spirit is the best example of not being jealous. His job is to unite God with Jesus. He sees the beautiful relationship with God and Jesus, which is his main source of joy. When God fills you with his spirit, you will be happy. You will have Jesus' nature and not a sinful nature; so, when you see a brother or friend with nice things, you will rejoice with them.

Diamond:

Did you know that diamonds are originally pieces of normal graphite that have minerals and after undergoing a huge amount of pressure, it turns into a rare diamond? When rocks are heated up or put under a lot of pressure, they can change dramatically. Pressures in life will form you to be like a precious diamond.

If your heart is willing to see the beauty in those around you, then you will see it; but, if your heart focuses on seeing the flaws in them, you will see that.

It is your choice and your attitude as to what you are going to focus on. Sometimes, like Lora, we learn in a hard way to make better choices in life. Challenges in life could be stepping stones for better changes in our life if we look at it that way.

You can look at the glass half full if you want and rejoice, or you can also look at the glass half empty and get mad. Your attitude is your mind set towards life.

The way you view things will determine how you behave and respond to it.

Do not let opposition destroy you. Instead, let your positive attitude empower you to overcome.

It is very sad to see many people respond with a negative attitude which leads them to violence, abusive crimes, to commit suicide, or to any other harmful attitude.

Be strong and never lose hope.

To fear the LORD is to hate evil; I hate pride and arrogance, evil behavior and perverse speech.

Proverbs 8:13

I went through a lot of trials and hardships in my life, but I refused to be depressed or feel sorry for myself because Jesus was telling me I am so proud of you my daughter for carrying the cross, going through the narrow path, and following me. Trials and pains helped me to feel God's presence during my time of prayer. I got to see him sitting with me. It is a great moment full of the best pleasure and true love that fulfills me more than any other fun or pleasure in this world. When you spend time in His presence, He will heal all your hurt and you will see His glory, which is part of God's life.

The Attitude Concerning Divorce:

Sometimes divorce in a family affects our attitude in a negative way. It causes a big disappointment in our lives, which effects our emotions and our security; but, you still need to know that your parents love you so much. Do not put many negative thoughts in your mind. It will affect your attitude with negative actions. God is telling you, "My child, do not be afraid of the unknown future. I am with you. I will never leave you or forsake you. I am your Daddy. I am holding your hands, do not be afraid."

Never be afraid of the unknown future because Jesus will always be with you. He said, "I will never leave you nor forsake you."

Capturing a positive attitude is a secret, which if understood, will be more valuable than all the wealth and fame this world has to offer.

When Others Attack Us with Their Bad Attitude:

When Others Attack Us With Their Bad Attitude:

Maybe you're telling me, "I bear a good attitude, but I face countless offenses and aggressions. It is hard to maintain a good attitude towards them, what I should do?"

Do not be overcome by evil, but overcome evil with good.

Romans 12:21

We respond with the attitude of forgiveness knowing that God is our Judge. This is the good attitude of putting God first.

Living in the world is like a vaccine. The world injects some germs into your body so your immune system becomes strong. When we are faced with anger, hurt, and offense, it is like the germs are penetrating our bodies. We need to fight in order to grow stronger with the Lord. Look at the offense as a vaccine to fight with the power of Jesus. We respond with the attitude of forgiveness. Do not look down on yourself.

Of course that is hard, but there are many things you can do.

I want you to use all the pain, suffering, distress and all the wrong actions that have been done to you for the better by helping those who have pain.

The Attitude of the Butterfly

Remember that the caterpillar inside the cocoon has to stay there in the dark and can't move or go anywhere for fun. It does this so that it can create stronger wings and be able to fly with great freedom as a beautiful butterfly, protecting herself. It is a great transformation. Always remember that the hard things and struggles in your life will make you stronger and more beautiful. You need to have the attitude that looks at things this way, not the attitude of self-pity. This kind of an attitude could hurt your emotions by causing you not to have a healthy way of thinking or healthy emotions. Many people act and react poorly because of their emotional damage. This type of person has a difficult time enjoying relationships. Never let the problems damage your emotions. You are going to have great wings like a butterfly. Remember, children that have everything and an easy life get spoiled and don't mature enough to carry any responsibilities. They never get a chance to be transformed into a beautiful butterfly with strong wings.

And when you stand praying, if you hold anything against anyone, forgive them, so that your Father in heaven may forgive you your sins.

Mark 11:2

For if you forgive other people when they sin against you, your heavenly Father will also forgive you.

Matthew 6:14

But I tell you that everyone will have to give account on the Day of Judgment for every empty word they have spoken.

Matthew 12:36

Trust in the LORD with all your heart and lean not on your own understanding; in all your ways submit to him, and he will make your paths straight.

Proverbs 3:5-6

Of course that is hard but there are many things you can do. I will focus on an important truth.

I want you to use all the pain, suffering, distress and all the wrong actions that have been done to you for the better by helping those who have emotional wounds.

I heard a great speaker who once said as a result of negative attitudes from brutal people; she gathered the deep and painful emotion inside of her and reversed it into a powerful action. This motivated her to study for a doctorate degree in counseling so she could help people avoid facing what she went through and encourage many people in order to bring help and healing to their emotions. Without her tragedy, she did not plan to do anything to help oth-

ers; but, she turned the negative attitude that attacked her into a selfless, positive one. She did not respond to the negative attitude with another negative attitude. She drew an opposite line to cross it and to stop it.

Children who share the same attitude as the speaker did, who allow that to happen, are leaders and history makers. They do not respond with another negative attitude creating equality. Instead, they oppose it with a crossing line to stop it. It is for this reason that they are leaders and history makers.

I remember that when I was a little girl I went through many challenges from many people who had negative attitudes. I realized how this pain affected me and similar children. With all my heart I turned all of the pain I had received into a passion for many children and developed a desire to help and restore relationships. I have also used this opportunity to become more humble. I want to help people choose the right attitude. I want to tell them that they are so precious, like a diamond because of all the huge pressure that have surrounded them.

Be strong. You can challenge all opposition. Look after one another so that not one of you will fail to find God's best blessings.

See to it that no one falls short of the grace of God and that no bitter root grows up to because trouble and defile many.

Hebrews 12:15

I chose to turn my sorrow from offenses into a humble attitude so that I can revenge from my real enemy because he is full of pride. When I humble myself, God will give me grace. He said He gives grace to the humble, but He opposes the proud.

Your Thoughts:

Do not get tangled in your own thoughts. When we do not have a peaceful attitude, we will fall under confusion. Test your thoughts. Do not agree with them when they are negative. Sometimes our thoughts are a big enemy when we choose bad attitudes that lead to wrong actions. Say no with a loud voice to any wrong thoughts that might affect your actions in a negative ways. Say, "No, I will be a strong leader." Learn to control your thoughts before they control your actions. Fill your thoughts with a good attitude. God is always watching your thoughts.

Many wrong attitudes come to us first in our minds. Do not communicate with fearful thoughts that make you believe negative things are going to happen. Instead, ask God to help you by sending his angels to you. Be alert and sacrifice to be a leader who leaves a great footprint. When we have negative thoughts, we open the door for bad things to happen. Negative thoughts come from fear and actual bad events that have happened in the pas; but, God said that he will compensate you. Know that He protects us with His angels. He will turn the bad things into good.

Learn to control your thoughts before they control your actions. Fill your thoughts with good attitudes. Forgive, forget and let go of the bad memories and fill your mind with only good memories. The pain of yesterday may keep us upset today; but we need to forgive, forget, and let it go. We cannot change the past, but we can change our attitude towards it. Do not let your reasoning or any logic deceive you

or hinder you from letting go of the bad thoughts. Do not let your painful thoughts bind you in your past. If you repeat painful thoughts, you will refresh, renew and continue them, but you need to completely let them go and not hold onto them. You need to put them in the trash for you to be able to enjoy your life. Do not blame yourself or others. Instead, learn lessons from the mistakes of the past. Use them to become stronger, which is a part of your growing. That is a greater attitude than blaming yourself for these mistakes. Repeating negative thoughts affect our mental health and our emotions. Try to do your best every day, and remember that no one is perfect.

Never make any decisions out of excitement or out of angry thoughts. This decision may not have a positive outcome that you could regret. Think for a few minutes before you talk and never talk while you are angry because you may hurt others. If you do, then when you are not angry anymore, you will regret what you spoke out of anger. You will realize that you said unkind words or made wrong decisions. We all learn from our mistakes so that we can make better choices in life.

If we have negative thoughts, we will not be able to take successful steps in life. Negative thoughts make us think and dream poorly.

Many wrong attitudes come to us first in our minds. Do not communicate with fearful thoughts, expecting bad things. Be alert and be willing to sacrifice to be a leader leaving a great footprint.

We always can ask for the grace of God and his mercy to help us.

Our Attitude Towards Those Who Are Different From Us:

Sometimes our attitude is negative and we reject those who are different from us in color, religion, or standard of living. Our attitude towards them never changes them, but can be negative. It will hurt them. And, if they get hurt they will vent this hurt in crimes, violence, and abuse. Our society will then become like a wild forest; not safe to live in. We will have to reap what we have sowed. Our attitude has a great impact to our parents, siblings, family, and friends.

"Live in harmony with one another. Do not be proud, but be willing to associate with people of low position. Do not be conceited."

Romans 12:16

As Christians, we have a big responsibility; we need to show the world our Christ, through our positive attitudes, for the world to believe in Jesus. We need to ask the Holy Spirit to give us positive attitudes.

But the fruit of the Spirit is love, joy, peace, patience, kindness, goodness, faithfulness.

Galatians 5:2

Focus in God and His Words as a Great Attitude:

Do not put any nice leaders or holy places above God or above the Bible. God will tell you, "I gave you my Bible to follow, not a man." He said in the Bible, "My sheep hear my voice and follow me." Ask God who you should follow. Many places make you feel like a perfect Christian, needing to do nothing. Sometimes many places or people tell you what you want to hear to be happy rather than the truth. Be very cautious. See what God's Word says. Going to holy places does not make you holy, but obeying God's commandments does.

Jesus overcame the negative attitudes that bother and hurt you. On the cross, He took them all. There is power in His blood. Just choose to obey God and have a positive attitude. He will certainly help you. Repent, confess your sins, cover yourself with His blood and ask Him to help you.

Believe in His promises.

He promises to give you peace, joy, a thankful heart, freedom, victory, power, forgiveness, humility, and everything you ask according to His will.

Jesus called us into His image. He will transform us into His image by His grace.

A Positive Attitude of Using Freedom in a Healthy Way:

You, my brothers and sisters, were called to be free. But do not use your freedom to indulge the flesh; rather, serve one another humbly in love. For the entire law is fulfilled in keeping this one command: "Love your neighbor as yourself. If you bite and devour each other, watch out or you will be destroyed by each other.

Sometimes we say, "I have freedom to do whatever I want." Well, freedom without obedience is a trap from the enemy. It steals our real freedom and puts us in bondage. On the flip side, when we say no to the enemy he can't steal our will.

Fear is a Negative Attitude:

God Sends His Angels to watch over us, surround us, and protect us.

Be strong and courageous. Do not be

afraid or terrified because of them, for the LORD your God goes with you; he will never leave you nor forsake you.

Deuteronomy 31:6

The LORD is my strength and my shield; my heart trusts in him, and he helps me. My heart leaps for joy, and with my song I praise him. The LORD is the strength of his people, a fortress of salvation for his anointed one.

Psalm 28:7-8

Attitude of judging others:

As human beings we do not have the right to judge anyone. It is also not our job to judge, even if we think that we are right in our judgments. It is still considered a negative attitude because we get hurt when people judge us, and when we judge others, we hurt them. Some people respond toward our mistakes by expressing their judgment through painful words, rejecting us, or treating us with anger. This attitude is painful and worse than the mistake itself. People who judge us make the same mistakes because of their negative attitude. We need to think of ideas to help others know how to avoid and learn from their mistakes and not judge them. Do not feel down or have low self-esteem when any one passes judgment on you.

Some people do good things so they can look good in front of people. They do not do these things out of a loving heart, desiring for you to do well. On the flip side, some people do good things in a hidden way and no one realizes every good thing they do, but they do it out of a loving heart and positive attitude.

For I know the plans I have for you, declares the LORD, plans to prosper you and not to harm you, plans to give you hope and a future.

Jeremiah 29:11

Praise be to the God and Father of our Lord Jesus Christ! In his great mercy he has given us new birth into a living hope through the resurrection of Jesus Christ from the dead.

1 Peter 1:3.

Jesus loves you so much. No one loves you like He does. He suffered agony on the cross to save your life. He died instead of you, so that you can live in Him and with Him.

Prayers:

"Lord, I repent for any wrong attitudes I might have had towards my sister, brother, parents, friends, or any one. Forgive me for any wrong words that have hurt you. I am taking power from Your blood that was shed on the cross for me in order to have victory. Give me grace to respond to others that come my way with Your loving attitude. Your love inside of my heart makes the impossible possible. For your sake, I will say, "I can do everything through Christ who strengthens me." I will spend time talking to You, seeing your beautiful face, and reading Your words so I can have Your glorious attitude. I will not give the Devil any more chances to steal my great attitude and replace it with his negative attitude.

Amen."

The Black Beetle:

I read an amazing fact about the giant palm tree and how the black beetle grows within the trunk. The insect lives there for years and then, it bores into the wood, and the tree starts to show signs of damage and becomes too weak to support itself. Then the wind causes the tree to fall down. The giant palm tree has a tiny insect growing inside, but everyone looks at it from the outside and says "wow, this is a very strong, giant tree. It bares beautiful fruits and everything seems great and suddenly, after years, this insect grows and breaks the giant tree. I see many families that are strong like this giant tree and then I hear that their lives fallen apart, unexpectedly .That is because they allow errors and negative attitude to grow within them. The small insect is a deception in your thoughts that tells you, "You are fine, you are against". It is just a tiny insect. But you must be careful; get the negative attitudes out of your life before they grow and a wind comes and destroys the beautiful tree of your life.

How to Obtain a Good Attitude:

If you put a sugar cube in water the water will be sweet because the cube will dissolve and be one with the water. In the same way, when we spend time with Jesus, He will live with us and you will share His attitude.

Spend time with the Lord daily, reading His words.

We need to repent for our wrong attitudes as a sin. Play worship music and continue to pray until you see that you have received power while you are worshiping and praying.

Do not give up or exult the power of the bad attitude. Instead, trust in the victory through Jesus' blood. He is greater than sin.

Choose friends with positive attitudes.

Love Jesus. Put His commandments first in your life. He said, "If you love me, you will obey my commandments."

Choose with all your heart to please God. When we sin, we insult Jesus and the power of His blood in front of the Devil, and in turn, we do the Devil's will.

Without Goliath, David's victory would have not existed!

Ask the Holy Spirit to convict you. This means that the spirit of God within you will grieve when you sin. When you see that, you also will see at the same time His power is in you to help you repent and correct your direction and your attitude. Without the Holy Spirit, you will judge yourself and that can be lies from the enemy because he is an accuser. The Devil judges you, accuses you, and makes you think that God is the one who is accusing you. God specializes in forgiving our sins if we choose to repent, depending on His blood and grace.

Do not look down on yourself.

Accept Jesus in your life and your heart as a savior. You can pray this prayer: Lord, I come to you today to hold your nail scarred hand accepting your love. Wash me and cover me with your precious blood. I repent for my sins. Help me with your grace to obey your commandments. I love you Jesus.

Your current attitude controls your words. For instance, if you have a negative attitude, then your words will be negative;

and if you have a positive attitude, your words will be positive.

Sometimes we believe that in order to be happy we must change everyone around us- just like what Lora had thought. The truth is that we instead need to change the way we look at matters by using a better attitude. Life would be a happier place if everyone focused on changing themselves rather than changing others. Another bonus is that if we are able to control how we react to others, rather than trying to control them, we will gain maturity.

It is very hard to change everyone around us, but we can learn how to respond to them!

\-

****

ATTITUDE IS A THINKING PATTERN THAT EFFECTS THE CHOICES IN LIFE.

Questions

- What does it mean to have a negative attitude?

- What does it mean to have a positive attitude?

- Is pride a negative attitude? How does it affect our lives?

- What should our attitude at home look like?

- How can you honor your parents? Write down some ideas.

- How can you create a better attitude with your sister or brother?

- How can hurt effect relationships?

- How should we respond when we face difficult times in our lives?

- How can we respond to a negative attitude?

- What should our attitude look like towards those who are different than us?

- How can you obtain a good attitude?

ABOUT THE AUTHOR

Welcome to Mona Lisa and her series of books on having a healthy heart. As you read her writings, you will quickly realize that she went through tremendous inner struggle while growing up, but, with a change of focus, was able to transform pain into something else. Now, she writes with a passion for children to have a loving and healthy relationship within their families.

Through her hardship, Mona shows us how to become victorious. She has been writing since 2001 bringing over 24 books for children and adults. Please read all of her books from the series on Heart to Heart. Mona Moubarek grew up as a second child in the Middle East. She has obtained a Bachelor Degree in Sociology, working toward Master's Degree from ACEI Beverly Hills, Ca. Mona has also received a Certificate of Counseling in 1995 from the California District.

She resides in Las Vegas, Nevada USA (since coming to the US for over 20 years) with her husband and children. English is the second language with Arabic as her first language. We look forward to releasing many of her books in Arabic!

HEART TO HEART BOOKS

This set of books focuses on nurturing sturdy spiritual and emotional values within children and families. They give building blocks for healthy relationships targeting what is most important deep down within the heart. Many books come with counseling manuals.

Look for more books on line at www.glorybound-publishing or contact Mona directly at email: monalisachurch@hot-mail.com.

A Gift for you granddaughter

Big Sister

Christmas Hat

Feel with me

Goodbye friend

I love you always grandpa

The angel of coins

The old bike

The red coat

The secret of the amazing zoo

The Spot

The Unhappy Elephant

Servanzo and Mac Miller

Welcome Friend

Why Mona Lisa

Your faith